STORIES FROM BRAMBLY HEDGE

WILFRED
TO THE RESCUE

Written by Alan MacDonald • Illustrated by Lizzie Sanders

Based on the world created by Jill Barklem

HarperCollins *Children's Books*

Jill Barklem created the world of Brambly Hedge in 1980 with
the classic books *Spring Story*, *Summer Story*, *Autumn Story* and
Winter Story, later followed by *The Secret Staircase*, *The High Hills*,
Sea Story and *Poppy's Babies*. These enduringly popular books
have sold more than 5 million copies, with the mice of Brambly
Hedge appearing on merchandise and in their
own animated television series.

Twenty-five years on, Brambly Hedge continues to delight both
children and adults. The classics are now joined by new stories,
recreating Jill Barklem's enchanting world for a new generation.

This edition produced for The Book People Ltd.,
Hall Wood Avenue, Haydock, St. Helens, WA11 9UL

First published in hardback in Great Britain by HarperCollins Children's Books in 2005
First published in paperback in 2005

1 3 5 7 9 10 8 6 4 2
ISBN: 0-00-776985-7

Visit our website at: www.harpercollinschildrensbooks.co.uk

Printed in Thailand

STORIES FROM BRAMBLY HEDGE

BRAMBLY HEDGE is on the other side of the stream, across the field, half-hidden under tangled roots and tall grasses.

This is the world of the little mice, Wilfred and Primrose, and their families.

The very best of friends, Wilfred and Primrose are always ready to share adventures.

Just like the time when the stream at Brambly Hedge burst its banks...

It had been raining for three days and three nights in Brambly Hedge. Wilfred's friend, Primrose, had come over to play.

"Rain, rain, rain," grumbled Wilfred. "Is it ever going to stop?"

That night there was a wild storm...

When Wilfred and his dad went out the next
morning they stared in astonishment.

"Where's the field gone?" Wilfred asked.

"By my whiskers! The water's almost up to the house,"
said his dad. "The stream must have burst its banks."

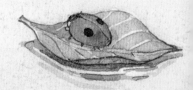

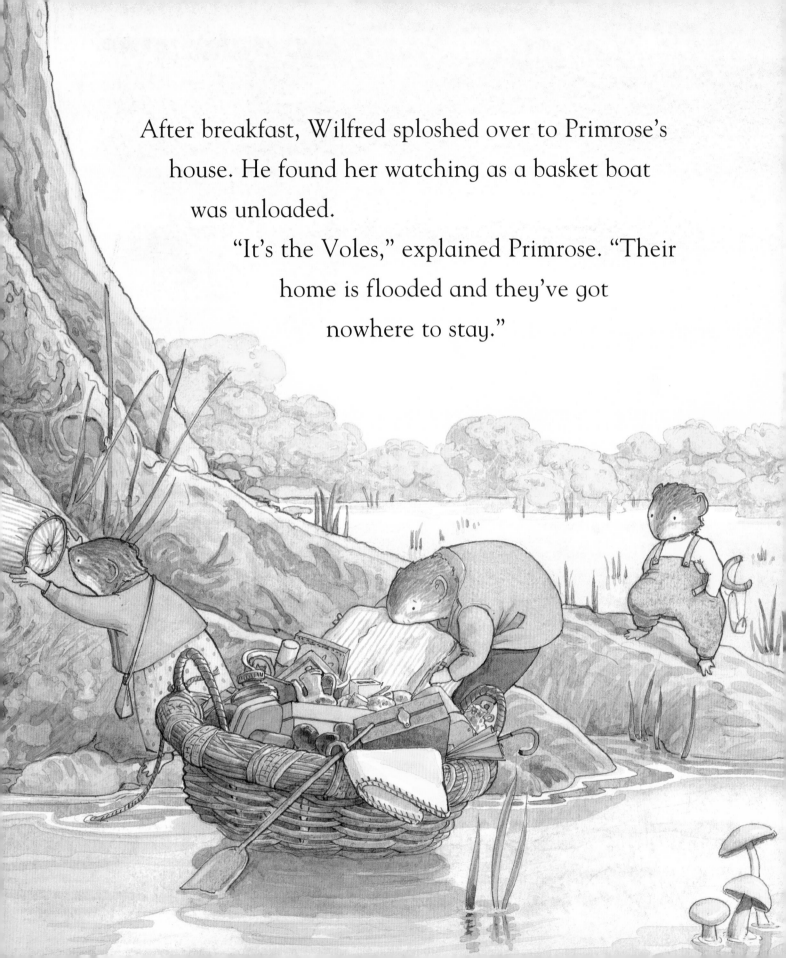

After breakfast, Wilfred sploshed over to Primrose's
house. He found her watching as a basket boat
was unloaded.

"It's the Voles," explained Primrose. "Their
home is flooded and they've got
nowhere to stay."

The Vole children
were called Horace
and Sissy.

"Are you going to
sleep at our house?" Primrose asked.

"Dunno," shrugged Horace.

Primrose's dad said that everyone
would stay with them until the
flood went down.

Wilfred helped to fetch food supplies from
the Store Stump on his dad's raft. They brought back
blackberry buns, cheeses and hazelnuts.

That evening they all crowded into the dining room
for a wonderful feast.

Later, Primrose suggested playing
a game of Hide and Squeak.
"Mind you look after Sissy," Mrs Vole told Horace.

While Horace counted to ten, everyone ran
off to hide. "Coming – ready or not!"
called Horace excitedly.

Horace found Wilfred and Primrose quite easily.
"But I can't find Sissy anywhere," he said.
"We'll help you look," offered Wilfred.

Sissy had found the perfect hiding place in the
basket boat, under her mum's green umbrella.
For a long time she waited. The boat bobbed
gently on the water making her sleepy.

Suddenly Sissy woke up. The boat seemed to
be moving. Peeping out, she saw that the rope
had come loose. The boat was drifting.
"Mu-um!" Sissy cried, but the wind
carried her small voice away.

Back at the house, Horace, Wilfred and
Primrose had searched every room.

"She's run off!" said Horace crossly.

Wilfred was staring outside. "That's
odd," he said. "Where's your boat gone?"

Horace turned pale. "Do you think Sissy
took it?"

Horace hid under the bed and wouldn't come out. "Go away!" he said.

"But what about Sissy? She could be in trouble!" urged Primrose.

Wilfred tried to think. "You could take the raft. She can't have gone far."

"Will you come too, Wilfred?" asked Horace in a small voice.

Primrose reluctantly agreed to stay behind in case Sissy turned up.

As dusk fell, Wilfred pushed the raft off from
the landing. Rain was falling again and muddy
water swirled around them. Wilfred steered
while Horace called, "SISSY!" into the gloom.

Alone in the boat, Sissy clung to her mum's
umbrella. She could no longer see the warm
lights of the house. She was cold and lost.
The current made the boat spin dizzily.

An old weeping willow trailed its branches in the water.
As the boat drifted by, Sissy tried to grab hold.
But she leaned out too far. The boat tipped up
and – SPLASH! – she tumbled over the side.

On the raft, Horace and Wilfred's throats were sore from calling Sissy's name.

Wilfred pointed at something on the water.

"Look! What's that?"

"Mum's umbrella!" said Horace.

"See if you can reach it."

As it bobbed past, Wilfred managed to catch the umbrella and draw it in. Something was curled up inside: a small, wet ball of fur. It blinked at them in surprise.

"Sissy!" cried Horace.

Back at the house, Primrose had explained
everything. Mrs Vole cried so much that
she needed to borrow three hankies. Outside in
the dark, tiny lanterns searched up and down.
"Look!" cried Primrose. "A light on the water!"

The light drew closer until, finally, they could see the raft.
On it were Horace and Sissy, with Wilfred steering them
safely home. A great cheer went up from everyone.

A little later they all ate toasted crumpets
round the kitchen fire. Horace told everyone that
he was probably the bravest vole in the world.

Wilfred bit into another crumpet. "The thing about
rescuing," he said, "is it makes you very hungry."